THE MIDNIGHT MOUSE

Mandy sat up in bed.

So did Amy. "What's that noise, Mandy?" she asked. "Is it my mouse?"

Mandy shook her head. "I don't know," she said. "I've never heard it before . . ."

*When you've enjoyed all the
Little Animal Ark books
you might enjoy two other series
about Mandy Hope, also by Lucy Daniels –
Animal Ark Pets and Animal Ark*

LUCY DANIELS

The Midnight Mouse

Illustrated by Andy Ellis

Hodder
Children's
Books

a division of Hodder Headline Limited

To Yvonne, who once saved a mouse
with an oven glove

Special thanks to Narinder Dhami

Little Animal Ark is a trademark of Working Partners Limited
Text copyright © 2001 Working Partners Limited
Created by Working Partners Limited, London, W6 0QT
Illustrations copyright © 2001 Andy Ellis

First published in Great Britain in 2001
by Hodder Children's Books

The rights of Lucy Daniels and Andy Ellis to be identified as the author
and illustrator of this work respectively have been asserted by them in
accordance with the Copyright, Designs and Patents Act 1988.

10 9 8 7 6 5 4 3

A Catalogue record for this book is available from the
British Library

ISBN 0 340 79135 7

Printed and bound in Great Britain by
Guernsey Press, Guernsey, Channel Islands

Hodder Children's Books
A Division of Hodder Headline Limited
338 Euston Road, London NW1 3BH

Chapter One

"We're not late, are we, Dad?"
Mandy Hope asked. "Amy will be
waiting for me."

It was Saturday morning and
Mr Hope was taking Mandy to
her friend Amy Fenton's house.

Mr Hope smiled as he drove
past Welford village green. "Don't
worry, love," he said. "The pet
shop won't run out of mice before
you and Amy get there!"

"I know, Dad," Mandy said with a grin. "But we want to get there early. Amy says it's going to take ages to find just the right mouse!"

Mandy loved animals. Her mum and dad were both vets.

There were always animals around at Animal Ark, their surgery. Today, Amy was going to buy a pet mouse. She'd asked Mandy to come and help her choose.

"Make sure you and Amy look for a healthy mouse, won't you, Mandy?" said Mr Hope, as they pulled up outside Amy's house.

"Yes, Dad," she said. "What should we look out for?"

"Well, a healthy mouse will have nice bright eyes, and clean fur," said Mr Hope. "Has Amy bought a cage for the mouse yet?"

Mandy shook her head. "No, she's buying *everything* today."

"Hamster cages are good for mice too," Mr Hope said, as Mandy undid her seatbelt. "They're large and roomy, and they have a wheel for exercise. But make sure the mouse can't squeeze through the bars of the cage, and escape. Mice are a bit thinner than hamsters!"

Mandy laughed. "I'll remember that, Dad!" she said.

Just then the Fentons' front door opened, and Amy came rushing out. "Mandy!" she shouted, "I thought you were *never* coming! Hello, Mr Hope."

Mr Hope waved at her. "Good luck with the mouse hunt

today, Amy!" he said with a grin.
Then he drove off.

Amy grabbed Mandy's hand.
"I'm so excited!" she said happily.
"I can't *wait* to get my very own
pet!"

Mandy grinned back. She
couldn't wait either! Life at Animal
Ark was too busy for Mandy to have
a pet of her own. But it was great
fun to share her friends' pets.

"Hello, Mandy," Amy's mum said, following Amy out of the house. "Let's go right away, girls. The pet shop will be very busy later on. It always is on Saturdays."

The pet shop was in Walton, the nearby town. As they drove along, Amy was so excited, she just couldn't sit still. Mandy just hoped that there were lots of mice to choose from.

And there *were* lots to choose from! Mandy could hardly believe her eyes. She stood in the pet shop and stared at all the glass tanks full of mice.

There were white ones, black

ones, grey ones, cream and brown
ones, all snuggled up together.

"Wow!" Amy said happily.
"Just look at all these lovely mice!"

The pet shop wasn't very
busy yet because it was still early.
So Mandy, Amy and Mrs Fenton
could take their time.

"Do you know what colour
mouse you would like, Miss?" asked
Mr Piper, the pet shop owner.

Mandy liked Mr Piper. Her friend Peter Foster bought dog chews from him for his pup Timmy.

Amy thought for a bit. She walked up and down, looking into the glass tanks.

Mandy looked too. She really liked the fluffy cream coloured ones. But then she liked the sweet little grey ones with pink noses, too. *And* the snowy white ones! She knew that *she* would find it *very* hard to choose!

At last, Amy stopped at the tank with white mice. "I'd like a white one, please," she said.

Mr Piper smiled and nodded. He carefully lifted the lid from the tank.

"Is there one special mouse you like the look of, my dear?" he asked.

Mandy and Amy looked into the tank, their noses pressed up against the glass.

"I just don't know!" Amy said. "They're *all* cute."

But Mandy was watching one little mouse in the corner. She scratched around, waving her long pink tail. Then she ran over and jumped playfully onto another mouse, who was having a snooze.

Mandy grinned and gave Amy a nudge.

The mouse saw Amy and Mandy looking at her through the glass. She padded over on her tiny pink paws, sat up on her back legs and stared right back at them, pink nose twitching.

Mandy looked at her shiny black eyes and smooth snowy coat. "She looks healthy," she said, happily.

"And she's got the sweetest pink ears. And look at her long whiskers!" said Amy. She looked at her mum. "Do you like her, too, Mum?"

Mrs Fenton smiled. "Yes, love," she said. "She seems very lively."

Amy turned to Mr Piper, then pointed to the mouse. "That's the one I want, please!"

Chapter Two

"Come on, Mousey!" Amy said proudly, as she carried her new pet into the Fentons' house. "This is your new home!"

Mandy laughed as she followed Amy inside. "You'll have to think of a proper name for her."

Amy nodded. She put the cage down on the living-room floor. The mouse was running around its new home, checking it out.

Mandy had told Amy what her dad had said, and Amy had chosen a cage with narrow spaces between the bars. It also had a wheel, and a little hut for sleeping in. They'd bought some bedding, some bags of food and a water bottle from the pet shop, too.

"Hello, Mousey," Mandy said. She bent down to look in the cage. The mouse was busy making herself a cosy bed.

"Can you think of a good name for her, Mandy? Amy asked.

"What about Snowy?" Mandy said.

Amy shook her head. "How about Fluffy?"

Mandy thought. "She doesn't *look* like a Fluffy," she said.

Amy looked at her mouse. "You're right," she said. She sighed.

"Never mind. We'll think of something!" said Mandy. "Are you going to take her out of the cage?"

Amy looked a bit worried. "I'm not sure how to hold her," she said.

"I've seen Mum and Dad pick

up mice at Animal Ark," Mandy
told her. "Shall I show you?"

Amy nodded.

"I'd better shut the door
first," said Mrs Fenton, coming
into the living-room. "I don't
want Miss Mouse running all over
the house!" she joked.

Carefully, Mandy opened the cage. She took hold of the mouse's tail with one hand, and slid her other hand under its furry little body.

"Doesn't it hurt her when you hold her by the tail like that?" Amy asked, chewing a fingernail.

Mandy shook her head. "No, not if you put your other hand underneath her. But my mum told me that you should *never* pick up a mouse just by its tail."

The mouse didn't seem to mind being picked up at all. She sat happily on Mandy's hand, cleaning her whiskers and looking at the girls with her bright eyes.

Mandy carefully passed her to Amy. The mouse sniffed at Amy's hand, and then tried to disappear up the sleeve of her jumper, squeaking as she went.

Mandy and Amy burst out laughing.

"I think she likes you, Amy!" Mandy said.

Just then, the phone rang. Mrs Fenton picked it up. Mandy and Amy were too busy playing with the mouse to listen to what Amy's mum was saying.

Mrs Fenton put down the phone. "Your uncle Jack's got flu," she told Amy. "He and your aunt Jenny were going to London today. They've got tickets for a show tonight and they've booked a hotel room. But now they can't go. So they've asked if your dad and I would like to go instead."

"That sounds lovely!" Amy said. "Are you going to say yes?"

Her mum shook her head. "I said we couldn't. There isn't time to find someone to come and look after you, love." She smiled and gave Amy a hug. "Never mind," she said. "We can *all* go another time."

But Mandy suddenly had a really good idea. She jumped to her feet. "Amy and her mouse could come and stay at Animal Ark tonight!" she said.

"Oh, yes, please!" said Amy. "We'd love that, wouldn't we, Mousey?"

"Well, that's very nice of you, Mandy," said Mrs Fenton with a smile. "But don't you think you'd better ring and ask your mum first?"

Mandy nodded, but she was sure her mum would say yes. She picked up the Fentons' phone and rang Animal Ark.

Emily Hope answered the

phone, and Mandy told her mum what had happened. "So can Amy and her mouse come and stay with us tonight, Mum?" she finished.

"Of course they can," Mrs Hope said. "I'm looking forward to meeting Amy's new pet."

"Oh, great!" said Mandy. "Thanks, Mum!"

Chapter Three

"So this is the famous mouse!" Mr Hope said as Amy and Mandy brought the cage into Animal Ark's kitchen. Mr and Mrs Fenton had dropped the girls off, on their way to London.

"Very sweet!" said Mrs Hope. "Have you come up with a name?"

Amy and Mandy looked at each other. "Not yet," they said together.

"What about Maxwell?" Mr Hope suggested, as he made some coffee.

Mandy and Amy burst out laughing.

"Yes, that's a great name, Dad!" Mandy said. "But it's a boy's name. This mouse is a girl!"

Mr Hope raised his eyebrows, then bent down and stared at the mouse.

The mouse stared back.

She twitched her nose at him, then ran into her hut.

Mr Hope grinned. "Oh, yes, so she is," he said. He went back to making his coffee.

Mandy and Amy carried the mouse's cage upstairs to Mandy's bedroom. They put it on Mandy's desk, and a few seconds later the mouse popped out of her hut. She had a good look round, and then sat down to have a wash.

"She knows she's somewhere different!" Amy said.

"I just wish we could think of a name for her," Mandy said, as the mouse began to clean her pink ears with her tiny paws.

"Mandy," said Amy.

"What?" said Mandy.

"No, I mean what about *Mandy*?" Amy said. "Mandy Mouse!"

The two girls laughed.

"Mandy Hope sounds all right, but Mandy Mouse is a bit funny!" said Mandy.

"Look, I think she wants to go to sleep," Amy said. The mouse had gone back into her hut, and was curling up in the soft bedding.

"Let's leave her to have a nap,"
said Mandy. So they tiptoed out of
the bedroom and went downstairs.

Mr and Mrs Hope were in the
Animal Ark office, doing some
paperwork.

"I've got a great name for
your mouse, Amy!" Mandy's dad

called. "How about Minnie?"

Amy frowned. "I like that name, Mr Hope," she said. "But this mouse doesn't *look* like a Minnie."

"Well, what about Mavis?" said Mr Hope.

"*Mavis*?" said Mandy and Amy together, shaking their heads.

"Molly?" said Mrs Hope.

But Amy shook her head again. "She's not a Mavis or a Molly," she said.

"What about Polly?" Mandy asked. "Or Sugar? Barbie? Susie?"

But Amy didn't think any of them were right for her mouse. "We'll just have to think a bit more!" she said.

Mandy and Amy decided to find some toys for the mouse to play with when she woke up. But they didn't know what she would like, so they asked Mrs Hope.

"Well, mice are the same as hamsters," Mandy's mum said. "They like tunnels, and things they can run and jump into. So the tubes from toilet rolls and kitchen rolls are good. So are small cardboard boxes. They can hide in them, and then chew them to bits!"

"Let's look around the house and see what we can find," Mandy said to Amy.

They found the middle of a

toilet roll in the bathroom bin, and Mandy's dad gave them some small cardboard boxes from the surgery. Then Mandy found a little ladder in her toybox, which had come from her old doll's house.

Mr Hope cooked tea while Mrs Hope took evening surgery at Animal Ark.

After they'd eaten, Mandy and Amy went back upstairs to see if the mouse was awake yet. They found her sitting up on her hind legs, nibbling seeds from her food dish.

"She's having her tea, too!" said Amy.

When she'd finished eating, Mandy and Amy had great fun showing the mouse all her new toys.

The mouse seemed to like them all. First, she climbed up and down the ladder.

Then she dashed in and out
of the cardboard tunnel.

She jumped in and out of the
boxes. Then she sat down to chew
them to bits!

Mandy and Amy played with the mouse until Mrs Hope came in and said it was time for bed. She brought in a camp-bed for Amy, and put it next to Mandy's.

"Now make sure you go to sleep," Mrs Hope said, as she turned out the light. "No sneaking out of bed to play with the mouse!"

"Goodnight, Mandy," whispered Amy. "Thanks for helping me with my mouse."

"It was fun!" Mandy said. She yawned. "Goodnight, Amy. Goodnight, Mousey!" Maybe tomorrow she and Amy would be able to think of a really good name for the mouse . . .

Squ-e-e-e-ak!

Slowly, Mandy opened her eyes. Was she dreaming? She'd just heard a very funny sound.

Squ-e-e-e-ak!

No, she *wasn't* dreaming.
There it was again! Mandy looked
at her bedside clock. The glowing
numbers told her it was very,
very, late – midnight!

Squ-e-e-e-ak!

Chapter Four

Mandy sat up in bed.

So did Amy. "What's that noise, Mandy?" she asked. "Is it my mouse?"

Mandy shook her head. "I don't know," she said. "I've never heard it before."

Squ-e-e-e-e-e-ak! The noise came again.

"Mandy, Animal Ark hasn't got a ghost, has it?" Amy asked.

She sounded quite scared.

"No, of *course* not!" Mandy said. But now she felt a tiny bit scared herself.

Squ-e-e-e-ak! Squ-e-e-e-ak! SQU-E-E-E-AK! The noise was getting louder and louder.

"What is it, then?" asked Amy, putting her hands over her ears. Then she gasped, her eyes wide. "Oh! It isn't my mouse, is it?"

Mandy shook her head. "No, it doesn't sound like a mouse at all!" she said.

They both listened hard.

Mandy switched on her bedside light and pushed back the

duvet. "I think it's coming from over by the mouse's cage though."

Her mum had told them not to get out of bed, but she just *had* to find out what the squeaking was!

"Is she all right?" Amy asked, looking worried. She got out of bed too and followed Mandy across the room.

Mandy looked into the cage. Then she began to laugh. The mouse was running round on her wheel. And every time the wheel went round, it squeaked. The faster the mouse ran, the louder the wheel squeaked!

Amy looked over Mandy's shoulder. "Oh, it's the wheel!" she said, and she began to laugh too.

Mandy opened the cage door, and gently lifted the mouse off her wheel. But as soon as Mandy put her down, the mouse jumped back on and started running again. Squ-e-e-e-ak!

"Let's give her some food," Mandy said. "Maybe that will stop her."

But the mouse didn't want any food. All she wanted to do was play on her wheel. She was enjoying her new game!

"Let's take the wheel out of the cage," Amy said.

But the wheel was fixed very firmly. Mandy was worried they might break it if they pulled it hard.

"What are we going to do?" Amy asked, putting her hands over her ears again. "We'll *never* get back to sleep with all this squeaking!"

Chapter Five

"I'll have to go and tell Mum and Dad," said Mandy.

Amy looked worried. "Will they be very cross?"

"I hope not!" Mandy said.

She crept into her mum and dad's bedroom and gave her dad's shoulder a little shake.

"Wh-a-a-h!" her dad said, waking up with a jolt.

That woke Mrs Hope up too.

"Mandy!" she said. "What are you doing up? Is something the matter?"

"Yes, Mum," said Mandy. "The mouse is keeping us awake!"

Mrs Hope looked a bit annoyed. "Is that all? If you leave her alone she'll soon settle down."

"Yes," Mr Hope agreed. "Now back to bed!"

"But, Dad, she won't stop running round on her wheel," Mandy told him. "And the wheel's making a horrible squeaking noise!"

Mr and Mrs Hope looked at each other.

"It can't be that bad, Mandy,"

said her mum.

"It is, Mum!" Mandy said. "We have to put our hands over our ears!"

Mr Hope yawned. "I'll come and have a look," he said, getting out of bed.

Before they even went into Mandy's bedroom, they could hear squeak, squeak, squ-e-e-e-ak!

"Goodness me," said Mr Hope, looking surprised. "That *is* loud!"

"I told you so, Dad!" said Mandy.

Mr Hope went to look in the cage. He began to laugh as he saw the mouse running round in the wheel as fast as she could.

"She should be in the Olympics!" he said. "I've never seen such a fast runner!"

"She's been running for ages now," said Amy. "She must be tired."

"She might be feeling a bit

upset," Mr Hope said. "After all, she's been to *two* different places today. When she settles down, she'll stop using the wheel so much."

"But how are we going to get to sleep tonight, Dad?" Mandy asked.

"I've got just the thing!" Mr Hope said, winking at them.

He went out and came back a few minutes later, carrying a can of oil. "This will do the trick!" he said.

Amy took the mouse off the wheel and held her, while Mr Hope put some oil on it. Then she put the mouse back in her cage.

They all watched as she hopped onto the wheel again. This time there was not a squeak to be heard!

"Phew!" said Amy and Mandy together.

"Thanks, Mr Hope!" Amy added.

Mandy gave her dad a hug.

"I think she'll go to sleep
soon anyway," said Mr Hope.
"Mice don't stay up all night.
They sometimes wake up and
move around a bit, but that's all."

"That's good!" said Amy.
"Because Mum says I have to keep
the cage in my bedroom at home!"

"Come on, you two," Mr Hope said. "Time for bed. I think we've had enough excitement for one night!"

Mandy and Amy jumped into bed, and Mr Hope turned out the light.

The two friends lay there listening hard, but they couldn't hear anything at all. At last they could get to sleep!

Chapter Six

Mandy opened her eyes and yawned. It was morning, and the sun was shining brightly into her bedroom. She looked over at Amy, but her friend was still asleep.

Mandy climbed out of bed. She didn't want to wake Amy up, so she tiptoed across the room to the mouse's cage.

The mouse was having her breakfast, nibbling a sunflower seed.

Mandy put her hand into the cage to stroke her.

As soon as the mouse had finished eating, she jumped onto her wheel and began running again. Mandy couldn't help giggling.

"What's so funny?" Amy said, sitting up in bed and rubbing her eyes.

"Mousey's on her wheel again!" Mandy said. She grinned at her friend. "We can't keep calling her 'the mouse', Amy! We'll have to think of a name soon."

Amy smiled. "I've *got* a name for her!" she said.

"Oh!" Mandy was very surprised. "What is it? When did you think of it?" she asked.

"I thought of it just before I went to sleep last night," Amy said. "I'm going to call her Squeaker!"

Mandy burst out laughing. "That's a great name, Amy!" she said. "It really suits her!"

Amy nodded. "And it'll always remind me of last night!" she said with a grin.

"Come on, let's go and tell Mum and Dad," Mandy said. She and Amy picked up Squeaker's cage, and went downstairs.

Mr and Mrs Hope were already

in the kitchen, having breakfast.

"So how's the mouse this morning?" Mr Hope asked. "She's not being too noisy, I hope?"

"Don't call her 'the mouse', Dad," Mandy said, grinning. "She *has* got a name!"

"She has?" Mr Hope said, raising his eyebrows.

"I thought you couldn't decide what to call her," said Mrs Hope.

"I made up my mind last night," Amy said. "I'm going to call her Squeaker!"

Mr and Mrs Hope smiled.

"That's a very good name, Amy," said Mandy's dad. He looked at Squeaker, who was having a drink of water from her bottle. "But I hope Squeaker never squeaks as loudly as her wheel did!"

In the afternoon, Mr and Mrs Fenton came to collect Amy and Squeaker.

Mandy and Amy were watching for their car. They went to the door to meet them, taking Squeaker with them in her cage.

"Hi, Mum, hi, Dad!" Amy said. "Did you have a good time?"

"Yes thanks, love, we did," said her dad, coming in through the door.

Mrs Fenton followed him in, and closed the door behind her. "And how's Miss Mouse?" she asked.

"*Squeaker's* fine!" said Amy.

Her mum and dad looked surprised. "*Squeaker?*" they said together.

Amy nodded. "That's what I'm calling her!" she said, taking Squeaker out of her cage to show them.

"That's a good name for a mouse!" Mrs Fenton said. "But how on earth did you think of it?"

Mandy and Amy looked at each other, and burst out laughing.

Mrs Hope came out from the kitchen. "Come in and have a cup of tea," she said. "And we'll tell you all about it!"

Do you love animals? So does Mandy Hope. Join her for all sorts of animal adventures, at Animal Ark!

The Playful Puppy

Mandy thinks Timmy, Peter Foster's new puppy, is adorable . . . but he chews things he shouldn't! Can Mandy help to find Timmy a less naughty game to play?

The Curious Kitten

Shamrock is a tabby kitten, with bright green eyes and tiger stripes. When Shamrock goes outside for the very first time, he soon runs into trouble . . .

The Brave Bunny

Laura Baker's pet rabbit, Nibbles, is scared of everything! But now he must be brave – he is very ill. Will Mandy's dad find out what is wrong with Nibbles?

Look out for more titles available
from Hodder Children's Books